BLESS the CHILD

Book Four
Pigeon Hollow Mysteries

Samantha Jillian Bayarr

ATTENTION READER: If you have not read the first THREE books in this series, this book will not make sense to you, as it is a continuation in the series. Please take the time to read Book One: The Amish Girl, and Book Two: Sins of the Father, for the best reading experience.

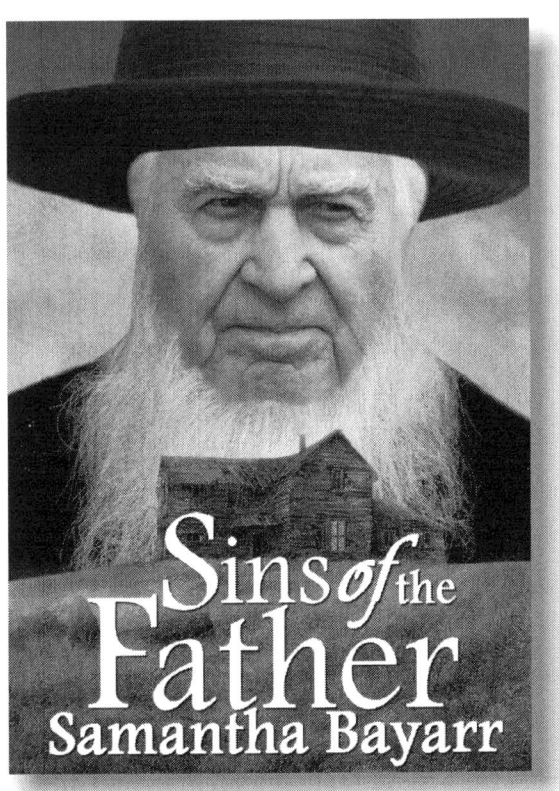

Sins *of* the Father

Samantha Bayarr

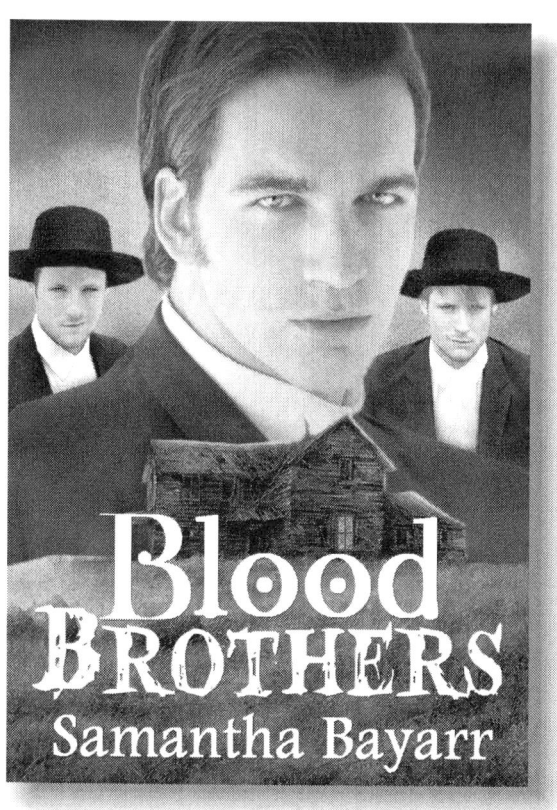

Blood
Brothers

Samantha Bayarr

A note from the Author:

While this novel is set against the backdrop of an Amish community, the characters and the names of the community are fictional. There is no intended resemblance between the characters in this book or the setting, and any real members of any Amish or Mennonite community. As with any work of fiction, I've taken license in some areas of research as a means of creating the necessary circumstances for my characters and setting. It is completely impossible to be accurate in details and descriptions, since every community differs, and such a setting would destroy the fictional quality of entertainment this book serves to present. Any inaccuracies in the Amish and Mennonite lifestyles portrayed in this book are completely due to fictional license. Please keep in mind that this book is meant for fictional, entertainment purposes only, and is not written as a text book on the Amish.

Happy Reading

Chapter 1

Amelia plucked the last cloth diaper from the wicker basket and lifted it to the clothesline, pinning it in place and then stepped back to admire the fruit of her labor. She was a proud *mamm* indeed. Before giving birth to little Gabriel, she had no idea that she could have so much love in her heart for such a tiny little human being. Nor did she ever think that he could go through so many diapers in a day. She giggled happily, and she picked up the basket and rested it on her hip. She looked up at the sun for a moment, taking note of what a beautiful summer day it was.

A sudden commotion from inside the house, followed by the high-pitched scream of her infant, sent a chill of terror through Amelia.

Amelia let the basket fall from her hip, as she pushed aside rows of diapers hanging from the clothesline, trying to push her way toward the house. Her feet felt stuck in mud so thick she could barely lift her legs, her muscles straining to push her to reach her infant. Her chest heaved as she ran the length of the yard toward her back door, intermittent cries escaping her lips, as her mind reeled with thoughts of her infant being in danger as he continued to scream.

"God, please let him be okay," she cried out, as she entered through the kitchen door. When she reached the inside of the house, the hair on the back of her neck served as a warning that something was not right. Gabriel suddenly stopped crying, but the commotion from the other room had not stopped. Chills turned her blood cold when she realized that someone was in the house.

Someone was in her baby's room.

Someone could be trying to hurt him.

Her gaze turned to the kitchen window and peered out to the driveway, making note that it was devoid of any vehicles, either horse-drawn or other. Being in such a remote area, Seth had tried hard to persuade them to install a telephone, but Caleb would not hear of it. He'd argued that just because they were not part of the community, that did not change their commitment to their Amish heritage, and a phone would hinder that commitment.

With no way to reach anyone, and her husband and brothers-in-law both working with him, no one was here to help her. Her mother had taken lunch to them at the construction site, and she would not return for at least another half hour—too late to help her.

Before she could think of what to do, a man—an *Englisher,* entered the doorway carrying her infant. Her heart slammed against her ribcage, and her throat constricted at the sight of her infant in the arms of the stranger. The man's expression turned from surprise at seeing her, to instant anger.

"What are you doing with my baby?" Amelia screamed. "Give him to me!"

The man gritted his teeth and narrowed his eyes "I'll give him back when you give me the money!"

She reached for her son, but he pulled back, causing Gabriel to cry.

Tears streamed down her face and she could barely breathe.

"I don't have any money," she sobbed. "I don't have any money; please give me back my son."

"You have money here, and I know it," he said. "I read all about it in the newspapers."

It slowly dawned on Amelia what he was talking about, and her heart sank at the reality that there was no money to give him.

"We don't have any money," she continued to cry. "Please, please," she bawled. "Give me back my baby; you're hurting him!"

"I'm not hurting the little fella," the man said as he jostled her son about carelessly. "We're just getting to know each other, but we're going to know each other real well if you don't get the money, because I'm taking him if you don't hand over the cash right now. You owe me!"

Chapter 2

"For the last time," the man said through gritted teeth. "Are you going to hand over the money in exchanged for the screaming kid, or am I taking him with me?"

"No!" Amelia screamed. "Please don't take him. I don't have any money to give you, but if I did, I'd give you all of it."

The man wandered over to the kitchen window and looked out as if waiting for someone—an accomplice, perhaps.

"I happen to have it on good authority, little Amish girl," he said. "You have a lot of money tied up in this land, so you're lying."

Amelia reached once more for her screaming infant, but the man jerked him away so hard, she worried that he'd hurt him if she didn't back off.

"At least let me calm him down," Amelia pleaded, trying to remain between the man and the kitchen door.

"Sit over there," he said, as he gestured with a tilt of his head to the side. "Sit over there in the corner—away from the door, and I'll bring him to you, but you better quiet him down," he ordered her.

Her heart melted with relief as her son was returned to her arms, even though she feared it was only temporary. She held him close to her and whispered prayers in his ear, hoping to accomplish two things. First and foremost, she needed to calm her infant, and secondly, she intended to plead with God to spare them the danger that she feared was to come.

"I'm going to need some diapers and some bottles," the man said, looking around nervously.

Amelia's breath hitched and she started to sob all over again. "Please, Sir. I don't know how to get you to understand that we don't have any money."

He charged toward her, anger in his eyes. "You're lying! I read about the robbery in the newspapers, and I know that you found the money hidden under the floorboards of your house."

"We turned the money in," she said. "They gave us a small reward, but my husband and his brothers used it to build their business. There's no more money left."

"You better come up with some," he demanded. "Even if you have to rob another bank, or I'm taking that boy with me." he said, pointing to Gabriel.

"No! I won't let you do it," she said, gritting her teeth. "I'll fight you to the death!" she surprised herself by saying.

He took a step toward her, causing her to jump instinctively.

"Oh, now you're threatening to kill me?" He asked. "Is this whole family full of murderers?"

"I'm not a murderer!" she said. "But I'm not going to stand by and let you take my child from me. I'll do whatever I have to!"

"You don't have a choice, Amish girl," he said. "Now tell me where that crying brat's diapers and bottles are so I can be on my way."

"Please, Sir," she pleaded. "He doesn't take a bottle. I nurse him."

"I guess he'll have to get used to taking a bottle until his mother decides she's going to trade him for the money," he said coldly.

"Please, no," she begged, sobbing.

"Does your kid have a car seat?" the man asked. "I can't hold him while I'm driving, and he'll be no good for ransom if he's all banged up."

Amelia gasped as she pointed to the opposite corner of the room where his car seat was. It had only been used to bring him home from the hospital since she had decided against a home birth. She sobbed as she wondered why she was helping him, but the thought of him taking Gabriel without the safety of the car seat filled her with absolute terror.

"I'm begging you not to take him. He'll die if I'm not there to feed him."

"Lots of babies take bottles," the man said, mocking her. "If you won't get me a bottle I'll get one for him. But we can avoid all this if you just hand over the money."

"I already told you," she sobbed further. "I don't have any money."

"Then I suggest you get together some bottles and diapers and clothes, because from the sounds of things, it's gonna be a while before you get me that money."

She jumped up toward him, pulling Gabriel close to her.

"Please, take me with you!"

Chapter 3

"Hey, it's me," the man said to the person on the other line. "Bring the car around, we're taking the kid!"

"No!" Amelia screamed.

She stood between the man and her child, who slept peacefully in his car seat, oblivious to the danger he was in.

The kidnapper reached out a hand and pushed her down into a chair. "Don't make me tie you up before I leave!"

"Please," she pleaded. "Take me with you so I can feed him. You won't get any ransom if my son is dead."

"Now you're talking the way I want you to talk," the man said. "I knew you had money."

"No!" She said. "You're wrong! We don't have any money, but I'm sure they can try to raise some. I don't think it'll be as much as you're asking for, but we can get you a little bit—a couple thousand maybe."

The man threw his head back and laughed heartily. "You think a measly few thousand dollars is going to satisfy me? I want the half a million that was stolen from the bank!"

Amelia collapsed to the floor and hovered over her son in his car seat and began sobbing uncontrollably. "I won't let you take him. I won't let you go without me."

"Fine, Amish girl," he said angrily. "Maybe the old man will pay more for the two of you."

"Are you talking about Zeb Yoder?" Amelia asked.

"Of course I am," he said. "I'm talking about the murderer. The one who murdered Rachel Miller, and the other two people—and who knows how many others."

Amelia felt her blood run cold through her veins at his statement. Who was this man? She looked deeper into his angry face, noting that he looked very similar to the way Seth had when she'd first met him. He had that same anger in his eyes, though he had no resemblance to the old man.

"Is your mother Rachel Miller?" Amelia asked sincerely.

"Rachel Miller is my wife's mother," he said. "Zeb Yoder killed her and put her in another woman's casket."

Amelia was all too familiar with the story of how the woman had gone to see Rose, Caleb's mom, and died from the tea that her father-in-law had laced with poison and sleeping pills. Rose had blamed herself for not thinking that the gift Zeb had given her could be tainted, and it was the cause of her friend's death. It had haunted her ever since that day when she'd unknowingly served her the poisoned tea. She'd blamed herself, and had to live with the guilt of that day, especially since she'd run away like a coward.

"She was the woman who was buried in my husband's mother's grave," Amelia said. "But if you think Zeb Yoder is going to give you a single penny for ransom for me and his grandchild, you're wrong! He doesn't care any more for me than he did for your wife's mother when she died because of him!"

"You sure seem to know a lot about my business! That *woman* was recently dug up," he said angrily. "Because your husband thought it was his mother buried there. But my wife's grandmother had filed a missing person's report when her mother had come up missing several years ago, and the detectives recently put the cases together and asked my wife to submit to a DNA test. Surprise, surprise, it was a perfect match. But why did you think she was *my* mother?"

"I just sort of assumed because of all these bodies showing up seemed to be women, and they seemed to be linked to Zeb Yoder in some way," she said quietly. "What about your wife's father?"

"Her father died before she was born," he said raising his voice.

"Do you know that for sure?" Amelia asked cautiously.

"Of course I know it because my wife told me that, and she's never lied to me. Why are you asking me these questions? Are you questioning my wife's morals?"

No, but I'm questioning yours!

"No, I'm not," she said, holding her hands up defensively. "It's just that my husband recently found out he had two brothers and it was because his father, Zeb Yoder, had fathered two other children with two other women–Amish women. We've suspected there were more siblings, and we especially suspected that the woman in the grave may have had a child with Zebedee Yoder. Your wife could be that child! If she's related to us, we'd be more than happy to help *both* of you."

"My wife is no relation to that murderer!"

Chapter 4

Amelia looked at the pregnant woman who'd entered her home to help the kidnapper, and knew immediately she was related to the old man. She could see a lot of Seth in her. She had the same darkness in her eyes that he'd had when they'd first met him. Despite the terror that ran through her, Amelia felt sorry for the young woman he called *Faith*.

"Get the baby's things!" he ordered the woman he'd claimed was his wife.

The young woman was clearly Amish, and he was an *Englisher,* and they seemed terribly mismatched. She supposed the woman may not have lived in a community since her mother's death.

"Please, Zack, I don't want to do this," she begged him.

He backhanded her, and she immediately raised a hand to her cheek to cover the welt, and began to weep.

Amelia was tempted to comfort the poor woman, but she had to remind herself of the immediate danger she and Gabriel were in.

Faith picked up the diapers and blankets that Zack had thrown at her, as she flashed Amelia a sympathetic look.

"What was that?" Zack questioned her. "You feeling sorry for that rich, Amish girl?"

He took a swing at her and she ducked away. "No! I just don't think this is the way to get the money."

"You let me worry about how to get the money for that kid you insist on having! I say we're taking her kid for ransom so we can pay for that one you're carrying!"

"No!" Amelia screamed. "I'll find a way to get you some money, but please don't take Gabriel."

Her lower lip quivered, and tears ran down her cheeks as she looked at his innocent face. He'd worn himself out crying, and was still sleeping peacefully.

"Please, God," she cried out. "Don't let them hurt my baby."

"God didn't help Faith's mother when Zeb Yoder was killing her. Why should he help *you?*"

"I'm sure God was with her in her final moments on this earth," Amelia said quietly. "Don't take it out on my baby what that man did. I had no control over that."

Zack leaned in close to Amelia and gritted his teeth. "I'm taking your kid for ransom. It's nothing personal. I just want my share of the money."

"I don't want that money, Zack, I've already told you that," Faith said. "Don't take her baby."

He slapped Faith again, her cry startling Gabriel, and he began to wail.

"Please," Amelia begged. "Let me comfort him."

"No!" Zack barked. "He's all strapped in, and we need to get out of here. We've wasted enough time already. Get his things, Faith, and we're going to walk out of here."

"What about me?" Amelia sobbed. "Please let me go with you so I can feed him."

"You better stay here so you can tell your husband we mean business," he said. "And if you try anything, I might have to shoot you!"

Amelia's breath caught in her throat, even though she hadn't seen a gun yet. That didn't mean anything; he could have kept it concealed.

She flashed a pleading look at Faith, and the woman made brief eye-contact with her, but it was enough for Amelia to know that she would help her.

She shook as she watched them leave her home, and she searched for a piece of paper to write a note. When she didn't see one, she tipped over the sugar bowl onto the table and scribbled the word *HELP* in the mess, and then crept out the door while Zack's back was turned to her. With him preoccupied with strapping the car seat into the back of the car, Amelia managed to slip around to the other side of the car unnoticed, praying the entire way that the door on the other side of the car was open.

The familiar sound of the clip-clop of horse's hooves filled her ears, and she knew it would only be her mother, but prayed the woman would intercept them, even though she knew there was nothing her mother could do to stop them.

Amelia crouched down at the back of the car and waited for Zack to walk around to the front so he could get into the driver's seat, and then she made her move. She threw open the back door and slid into the seat and slammed the door before he knew what was happening.

He looked at her from over his shoulder, screaming for her to get out of the car, but Faith interrupted him.

"Close your door, Zack!" she urged him. "Someone's coming and we're gonna get caught!"

Zack took his eyes off Amelia long enough to look toward the end of the long driveway, where the horse and buggy had just pulled in.

"Is that your husband?" he asked.

"I don't know who it is," she said, knowing he could not see who was in the buggy at this distance.

"Let's go before we get caught and you go to jail," Faith urged him.

Amelia didn't know if the woman was on her side or not, but she wished it had been Kyle's truck that had pulled in instead of the horse and buggy.

Zack jumped into the car, grinding the tires in the gravel driveway as he sped down the lane toward the buggy. He veered off the path when he neared the horses, and Amelia pressed her face against the glass, praying that her mother had seen her in the car.

Chapter 5

Abigail steered the horses out of the way of the oncoming car that came barreling down her daughter's driveway.

"Melia," she cried as she watched her daughter fly by in the speeding car. She hadn't missed the look of terror on her little girl's face, and Abigail knew she was in trouble.

Had something happened to the baby? The couple who were in the front seat of the white BMW were not any of the normal drivers for the Amish, and she wondered where they would be taking her daughter and grandson in such a hurry. Amelia would have had no way of contacting them, so it just didn't make any sense. Turning around as they sped away, she noted the vanity plate read: *HSR-DDY.*

Then a thought hit her, and she wondered if the old man was behind this in some way.

She slapped the reins to move the horses toward the house faster. She had no idea what she would do once she got there, but she hoped, perhaps, that her daughter had left a note that would explain.

As she approached the house, she ran up to the open kitchen door. Seeing the message written in sugar on the table, she scrambled back out of the house and hopped into the buggy.

She urged the horses faster down the road to the construction site where her son-in-law and his brothers were putting a roof on a new house.

When she reached the site, she didn't even bother to slow the horses before jumping out of the buggy. She ran fast to reach Caleb, screaming to get his attention. He dropped the tools in his hands and ran to her, placing a hand on each of her arms to calm her.

"What's wrong?" He asked.

"Did Amelia make arrangements to have some *Englishers* take her and the baby somewhere today?" She asked, trying to catch her breath.

"No, why? What happened?" he asked.

"When I drove back to the house after bringing you boys your lunch," she said, still out of breath. "She was speeding away in a white BMW, and the baby was with her. But when I went into the house, I saw that she'd scribbled the word *help* in a pile of sugar on the table."

"What are you talking about?" He asked. "That makes no sense."

"I don't know how she would've gotten word to the people that were driving her, but when I saw them go by, she had her face pressed to the glass, and I could see she'd been crying. I hope nothing has happened to the baby."

"Maybe we should go to the hospital and see if they went there. But why wouldn't she have taken the time to write a proper note explaining where she was going?"

"I don't know, but let's go."

By this time, Seth and Kyle were at his side, and had heard the whole thing. Seth offered to put away all the tools and then meet them at the hospital, while Kyle offered to drive them.

Seth tied up the buggy at the site deciding it was best to leave the horse there for now.

The three of them piled into Kyle's truck and he sped off toward the hospital, which was about eighteen miles down the road.

None of them said another word the entire ride there; tensions were high. When they reached the hospital, Kyle let Abigail and Caleb off at the emergency room entrance, and went to park the truck. When he made his way to the entrance to the hospital, Abigail and Caleb were running back out.

"She's not in there!" Caleb said.

"They said it's been a slow day for them. The nurse told us they've only had two senior citizens come through today, and no one with a baby."

"Where can she be?" Kyle asked.

"I think we need to go to the police," Abigail said. "I told you Amelia looked like she'd been crying, and that car was driving way too fast down the driveway. I don't know why they were in a hurry, but I've got a bad feeling about this."

They all got back in the truck and drove down to the police station another several miles down the road.

"What are we going to say when we go in there?" Kyle asked.

"I guess we need to tell them all we know," Caleb said. "Is there anything you left out, Abigail?"

"I noticed the license plate, and both the driver and the woman in the front had dark hair, but they were going so fast and I was busy trying to get the horses out-of-the-way so they wouldn't hit them, that I didn't get the best look at them like I should have."

"What was the license plate?" Kyle asked.

"It was HSR – DDY," she said.

"Hoosier Daddy--who's your daddy?" Kyle said with a sigh. "Not very original is it?"

"I didn't know that's what that meant," Abigail said. "But I guess it makes sense now that you figured it out."

"One thing's certain," Caleb said, as they entered the police station. "It should make it easier to find them."

"Let's pray that it is so," Abigail said.

Chapter 6

"I'm afraid I have some bad news for you," the officer said as he entered the lobby where the four of them had been sitting waiting to hear the results of the record search for the license plate.

"Let me guess," Kyle said. "The car was stolen!"

"I'm afraid so," the officer said. "The owner reported it missing yesterday afternoon. But the good news is, we have officers in the area, and we'll see if we can find them."

"I'm afraid you can probably search the area all day long and won't find them," Kyle complained. "They've obviously ditched the car and have found another one."

The officer turned around as another officer called him back to a locked door. "Excuse me just a moment," he said to them. "I'll be right back."

Caleb paced back-and-forth in the lobby, while Kyle watched out the window at Seth, who was leaning against his car and smoking a cigarette. He'd been so good about not smoking, and here he was, out there on his second one already. It was obvious he was having trouble handling the stress.

When the officer returned, his face did not look as if he was bearing any good news. "They found the car abandoned in an alley about 12 miles from here," he said. "We can search the area, but my guess is that they've stolen another car in order to get where they need to go. That means that if we get another report of a stolen car, we'll be checking it out to see if they fit the description of your wife's abductors."

Kyle went to shake his hand, and thanked him.

"I'm afraid I have some worse news than that," the officer said sincerely.

Caleb shook, and Kyle could see he was thinking the same thing—that they found evidence like blood or something in the car.

"Maybe you folks should have a seat." He gestured back to the chairs where they were sitting in the lobby, and everyone sat down robotically; the room was so quiet it was almost deafening.

"Please just tell us everything," Kyle pleaded. "No matter how bad it is; we need to know."

"Well, I guess you need to know what you're dealing with," the officer said. "We just got word that your father has escaped again."

"What?" Caleb said, jumping up from his chair. "When did he wake up from his coma?"

"Apparently he just woke up yesterday and they were getting ready to move him back to the prison, and he managed to escape again."

"We don't think he's going to make it far, because he's weak from being in a coma for so long."

"He isn't dumb enough to go back to his house; he knows that's the first place you'll look."

"We doubt he'll go back to his house this time since we found him there the last time," the officer agreed. "I imagine he's going to hide out somewhere until he feels it's safe, or he could even be planning on leaving the state."

"If he's holding my wife hostage, then…" he couldn't finish his sentence, and Abigail pulled him into a hug.

"We'll be patrolling the area just in case. I'm afraid I don't have anything else for you, but we'll keep an eye out for your wife and your son. In the meantime, my suggestion is that you go home and prepare yourself for a possible ransom note. I imagine your father's freedom is going to be the price he'll be asking for."

"What about the couple I saw driving her away from the house?" Abigail asked.

"They might be working together," the officer said. "There's no way to be sure, unless we get word from someone, either in the form of a ransom note, or a phone call."

"Now we need to be on the lookout for the old man on top of everything else," Kyle said soberly.

"You don't think he'd hurt his own grandchild, do you?" Caleb looked at his brothers, tears welling up in his eyes. "After all he's done, I just can't trust him anymore. It seems to me, that our father is the type of man that would hurt even an innocent baby if he got in his way."

"So who do you suppose we should be looking for: your father?" Abigail asked. "Or Amelia?"

"Unfortunately," Kyle said. "I'm afraid we're going to find them in the same place."

"Do you really think he would hold his own grandchild hostage for his freedom?" Caleb asked. "It doesn't make sense."

"It makes perfect sense," Kyle said. "Do you forget that he held my mother hostage to keep his secrets hidden from the community? He did it to keep his standing here, and let's not forget his being arrested interrupted his last hope of getting the Bishop to listen to his confession and welcome him back. I think that's all he's wanted all along."

"You think so?" Caleb asked.

"Let's not kid ourselves," Kyle said angrily. "The Bishop was not going to welcome him back. He only wanted the confession."

"Perhaps if we could somehow get the Bishop involved and get him to promise our father amnesty, perhaps we can put an end to all of this."

"It's possible that might just work," Caleb agreed. "The only problem is; how do we get the Bishop to go along? You remember he had all of us shunned, and he doesn't want us in his community. He certainly doesn't want our father to be a part of the community. I'm not sure at this point that he would even agree to listen to his confession so he can be forgiven."

"Caleb," Seth said, stepping into the conversation. "I thought forgiveness was what the Amish were all about? Kyle and I didn't grow up Amish like you did, but if there is no forgiveness in the community, where do we stand?"

"I'm not sure," Kyle said. "But right now, I think that's our only hope."

Chapter 7

"Why are we switching cars?" Amelia asked her abductors. "Why would you leave your car here in this alley? Aren't you afraid someone will steal it?"

Zack chuckled at her. "You naïve little Amish girl, we stole that car!"

"I didn't know he was gonna steal the car," Faith said trying to defend her innocence. "And I didn't know we were gonna take you or your baby."

Zack raised his hand toward her, and she ducked.

"Shut up Faith! Shut up now!"

"It's not too late to turn back and stop all this, Zack," she pleaded with him. "You told me those people owed you money. I didn't know you were going to resort to stealing cars and kidnapping. I don't want my baby's father to go to jail."

"No one is going to jail. I told you to shut up!"

They all piled into a rusty gold Pontiac that smelled of dirty feet and cigars inside. Amelia coughed at the smell when she got in, pushing aside trash that was on the floor at her feet. She tried locating the buckle to the seatbelt so she could strap Gabriel's seat in, but it was buried deep beneath the sticky, gummy, dirt-stained seat.

She winced as she put her hand down between the seats and felt amongst sticky dirt to locate the other side of the buckle. When she pulled it out, her fingers were black with dirt. She wiped them on the already dirty upholstery, realizing that they weren't going to come clean. It wasn't important in the grand scheme of things, but it certainly made matters worse. She shrugged it away and strapped him in, thanking God that he hadn't yet woken up.

Zack tried several times to start the car, but it stalled each time, and Amelia prayed it wouldn't start and they would get caught. On the fourth try, it started, but then backfired, causing Gabriel to startle in his sleep. It started on the next try, and Zack revved the engine. Gray smoke billowed out from the back of the car and filtered into the windows, causing Amelia to cough.

When the car took off, she was grateful for the breeze that blew out the exhaust smell from the car.

Zack followed the same path leading almost directly back to her home, and she thought for a moment he'd changed his mind. When he turned into the driveway of the old man's farm, she feared that she was in bigger trouble than she originally thought.

"Why are we turning in here?" Amelia dared to ask.

Zack chuckled. "I thought it would be pretty smart to hide you directly under their noses. Besides, I already told you that old man owes us for what he did the Faith's mother!"

"And I already told *you*," Faith complained. "No one owes me anything, and I don't want anything from that old man! My *mamm* has been dead for a lot of years, and I've had a long time to get used to it—for plenty of years before I met you."

He grabbed her arm and shook her, gritting his teeth as he swerved the car, causing Amelia to brace herself against the door.

"And I told you that you had no life before you met me!"

Faith buried her face against the window and began to cry quietly, but Amelia could see from her shaking shoulders that she was crying. It was tough for her not to feel sorry for the woman, knowing how lucky she'd been to find such a gentle and caring husband who would never raise his voice or a hand to her. But no matter how she felt about Faith, she had to keep her head about her and not get emotionally involved. She had to remember to keep her wits about her in order to keep herself and her son safe.

Their very lives depended on it.

Chapter 8

"Have you got any more bright ideas?" Seth asked his brothers when they left the Bishop's porch. "That old man wouldn't even let us in."

"I can hardly blame him," Caleb said. "He doesn't want to get involved, and I understand that even if I don't like it."

"I thought men of God jumped at the chance to minister to sinners—especially murderers!" Seth argued.

"Well, one thing is certain; I can't stand around here waiting for my family to either be returned to me, or get word that they're no longer alive."

"Maybe we need to see if we can figure out where the old man is hiding out," Kyle said.

"He had so many mistresses, it's possible he has places he could stay that we don't even know about," Seth said with disgust.

"Who do you suppose the couple could be that took her?" Kyle asked. "Abigail said they looked like they were about our age. Who do we know that would do such a thing?"

"No one! But the thought had crossed my mind that we could have a fourth brother," Seth said with a half chuckle. "Maybe he has a chip on his shoulder like the old man, and he wants revenge!"

"Well, there was another body that turned up. Why don't we ask Aunt Rose to tell us a little more about the woman who was buried in the grave that was supposed to belong to my mom," Kyle said. "Maybe she had a child, and that child could be the one we're looking for!"

"That's a long-shot," Seth said. "But it's all we have to go by right now."

They went directly back home, knowing that all three of their mothers were at the main house waiting for any word about Amelia and Gabriel.

"Rachel and I weren't the best of friends," Rose said sadly. "We were classmates, but we were never really friends. She and her mother had come from another community, and they just didn't have any family here, and they never really tried to fit in. They were only there for the last year or so of school, and then they moved away. When she began to work at the bakery many years later, we started talking and realized we knew each other when we were young. I do remember a young girl going to visit her a couple of times at the bakery. She had dark hair, and she would be about the same age as you boys. I don't remember her since she was only there for a minute or two to drop something off to Rachel. At the time, I asked her if it was her daughter and she said she was, and that her husband had died before her daughter was born."

Kyle ran out to his truck and grabbed a stack of newspapers and brought them into the house. He flipped through them furiously until he came to the article about Rachel Miller.

"Look here," he said pointing to the newspaper. "It says here she left behind a daughter named Faith. Faith Miller. And she's our age!"

Kyle turned to his aunt. "Why did she come to visit you that day if the two of you weren't close?"

"When she dropped in that day, she said she had something weighing on her mind—a confession of sorts. We never did get around to talking about what it was she wanted to say because the tea caused her to feel dizzy, and when she went to use the bathroom, she stumbled and fell on the table. She died instantly."

Rose began to cry, remembering that day she'd had an upset stomach and didn't think she could drink or eat anything, so she hadn't even taken a sip of her tea yet. When her friend stumbled, she knew then it was because of the tea Zeb had given her as a gift.

Seth jumped up from his chair. "I'd be willing to bet her confession had something to do with her daughter and the old man. He must be her father!"

"You mean we could have a *sister?*" Caleb asked.

"I think it's possible," Seth said. "All we have to do is find this *Faith Miller,* and I'd be willing to bet we'll probably find Amelia and Gabriel."

"I thought you gave up betting," Kyle teased him.

"Not when it's a sure thing!" Seth admitted.

"It might not be that simple," Kyle said. "What if she *is* his daughter, and she's as bad as he is and they're working together? You have to admit the timing of Amelia being taken, and the old man escaping is probably not a coincidence."

Seth pulled out his cell phone and called the police detective listed on the business card they'd gotten earlier. He abruptly hung up the phone, frustrated that he'd had to leave a message because the detective was not available.

'We can't just sit here and do nothing,' Seth said. "How do we find this Faith Miller? Maybe someone at the bakery would know. What was the name of the bakery, Aunt Rose?"

"It's called The Brick Oven, and it's right downtown in Hartford."

Seth pulled out his keys. "Who's with me?"

"I'll go," Kyle offered. "You stay here, Caleb, in case we get word. I'll leave my cell phone with you just in case."

"That won't do me any good," Caleb complained. "I don't know how to use it."

"I do," Selma spoke up. "You boys be on your way. We'll stay here, and I'll call you if there's any word, and you do the same."

They each kissed their mothers goodbye, and Seth flashed his brother a sympathetic look. He hadn't been part of the family for very long, but he was already emotionally attached to every one of them, and Amelia's and his nephew's disappearance hurt him more than he could ever let on.

Chapter 9

Amelia felt awkward feeding Gabriel with Zack so close nearby, but he wouldn't allow her to go into the other room to feed him in private. Faith had found her a throw-blanket that was tossed over the sofa so she could at least keep herself hidden from the evil man.

He'd joked with her several times, stating how funny it was that he should hide her right under the noses of her own family, but knowing the history of her family, they were more likely to start their search on the old man's property.

She would never tell him that.

Amelia was hoping to get a moment away from Zack so she could talk to Faith about her hunch that they were related. She felt certain Faith was her sister-in-law, and she hoped the information would get the woman to be completely on her side. It was obvious to Amelia that Faith wanted no part in her husband's crimes, but in her condition, she probably felt there was no other way but to go along with the unreasonable man.

Zack had found jars of fruits and vegetables tucked away in the pantry that the old man had canned, and he was preoccupied at the moment with eating, though he hadn't offered any to the two women, least of all his pregnant wife.

Faith sat near her. "You know, he wasn't always like this," she said quietly. "When we first met, he was very gentle and very kind. He was so romantic, I married him only one week after meeting him. But now I wonder if I should've thought that through."

Amelia reached a hand out and touched her cheek that still boasted a deep welt from where Zack had slapped her.

"I'm afraid you're going to have a bit of a black eye," Amelia said gently.

Her lips formed a thin line, and tears welled up in her eyes. "It wouldn't be the first one. I told myself after that first one I wouldn't stick around for another," she said, as she patted her belly. "But this little one here has changed all that."

"Well, if anything," Amelia said as kindly as possible. "That little one should bring the two of you closer together."

Faith lifted a hand and waved it at her. "Oh, don't mind him," she said, defending him. "He's just nervous about all the money the baby's gonna cost us. It's been worse since he lost his job."

"There's a lot of things that he can do. I'm sure my husband and his brothers would've been more than willing to let him work with them. But now, well, after what he's done, I just don't know. I couldn't speak for them."

"People like you don't help people like us," Faith said, lowering her head in shame.

"You know better than that!" Amelia said to her. "We're both Amish. Weren't you raised Amish?"

"Only slightly; my *mamm* was too ashamed to be a part of the community since I was born out of wedlock."

"I thought Zack said that your father died before you were born."

"That's what she used to tell me, so I tell everyone else that to keep from shaming her—especially now that she's gone. But we got in a big fight one day before she disappeared, and she admitted the whole thing to me. She said she'd needed to get it off her chest for a very long time, and she felt relief after telling me the truth. But there's no forgiveness from the community for her since we couldn't be part of the community because of it. I know the Amish ways are about forgiveness, but sometimes those ways come with flaws—flaws that don't fully forgive a person's mistakes."

"I know what you mean," Amelia said. My husband and I were both shunned because of the mistakes that our parents had made, and we were just innocent children. We fell under the ban because of them, and at that time, we really could've used the community's help. But they turned their backs on us, mostly out of fear, but my husband feels that was no excuse."

"I agree with your husband."

"We know now that had more to do with the Bishop than the people in the community, because we have a lot of friends within the community."

"That's good that you have that," Faith said. "But that won't help us."

"Let me help you," Amelia pleaded with her.

"After what we've done to you, why would you want to help me?" Faith asked, tears in her eyes.

"Because I think you're my sister-in-law!"

Chapter 10

Zack charged toward Amelia, and she started to wince, but caught herself. She was tougher than this. She knew if she showed fear, it would be all over for her.

He raised a hand to her. "I told you my wife ain't related to that murderer!"

Amelia stood her ground. "She looks so much like my brother-in-law they could be twins! That would make her my sister-in-law, and you can't change that if it's a true fact."

He raised his hand higher, but she kept herself from cowering.

"You think I'm afraid of you slapping me in the face the way you smack your wife around? I shot a man when I was ten years old, and then I spent the rest of my childhood in an orphanage, so I know how to fight!"

Zack backed away. "You're not worth it. I won't get much ransom for you if I send you out with a black eye."

Amelia slowly let out the breath she'd been holding in so he wouldn't hear, as she watched him go back over to gobbling a Mason jar of peaches. She sat back down next to Faith and kept quiet, not wanting another confrontation with him.

When he finished, he picked up a pad of paper and a pen from the kitchen table and tossed it at her.

"Let's get to writing that first ransom note!"

"Why me?" she asked.

"I figure if it's in your handwriting, your family will know you're not hurt or anything," he said.

When he turned his back, Faith whispered in her ear. "He didn't finish school, so he doesn't read or write so good."

That was good news to Amelia, her mind immediately reeling to the possibilities of codes she could encrypt into the message. She'd have to be careful, figuring he'd probably have Faith read it before it went out, and she wasn't entirely sure if the woman would let a blatant cry for help pass by her without telling her husband. Even if she wouldn't say anything, her expression might give it away, and Amelia wasn't about to take that chance.

As Zack relayed to her what to put in the note, she was busy trying to figure out how to word it to send her husband a message within the message. When they were kids, they'd used homing pigeons to communicate, and they'd developed a way to send an extra message that only they knew by making certain words less obvious by using upper-case letters to spell out another word. It had been fun when they were kids, but she'd had no idea then that such childhood play could one day save her life.

> caleb,
> Please go to sister Felicia At
> fenwIck hall (THe oRph -
> Anage) and have her release
> my inheritanCe tHat was
> LEft for me. ransom is to be
> half a million dollars.
> more instructions later
> ~Amelia

Zack snatched the note from her and handed it to Faith so she could read it to him.

"Who's Sister Felicia, and why does she have your money? I thought you said you had no money!"

It wasn't a lie, but she knew she would have to skate around the truth to convince him the money was there.

"I had money that the state is supposed to grant to me on my twenty-first birthday from my parents' estate, but I'm sure they'll release it early if it's an emergency. When I left, I'd asked them to hold it until then, since I didn't want the money. I thought it was from the robbery. I didn't figure I would ever go back for it."

"How much is it?" he asked, his eyes lighting up with greed.

"Two hundred fifty thousand!" she answered.

His eyes lit up even brighter, and the corners of his mouth turned up into a sickening smile.

She'd meant *pennies,* but he didn't have to know that. The gleam in his eyes let her know he was falling for it, and she would not have to lie to convince him, rather than confessing it only amounted to twenty-five hundred dollars.

His expression quickly changed to anger. "That's a start, but it's not nearly enough!"

Faith tucked her arm in his and smiled weakly.

"That's more than enough, Zack. Let's not be greedy!"

"I'm not being greedy! I want what's coming to us!"

I have a feeling you're going to get exactly what's coming to you!

"After dark, you can walk around and put the note on the door of her house."

Faith looked nervously between her husband and Amelia, fearing the woman would not be alive by the time she returned.

"That's a long walk, Zack," she complained. "Will you go?"

"If I go," he growled. "I'm tying the two of you up!"

"Why me? I'm your wife!"

His gaze traveled between the two women.

"I don't trust her not to convince you to let her go," he growled. "Ever since you got pregnant, you've become weak, and she's already put ideas in your head that she wants to help you, and you're falling for it. So what's it going to be? You delivering the ransom note, or am I tying the two of you to a chair?"

"Tie us to a chair!" Amelia said with a bit of an edge in her voice. "She doesn't need to be walking all that way in the dark in her condition!"

He chuckled angrily. "Have it your way, Amish girl."

Chapter 11

Seth walked out of the *dawdi haus* that he'd agreed to share with his brother, Kyle, until Amelia and the baby were returned home safely.

He needed a cigarette, and he'd had to wait until Kyle was asleep to avoid reprimand from him. He'd made promises to quit, and he had been truly trying, but his tension was so high right now that he needed one, and he needed it in the worst way.

He crept out the door and walked far enough up into the driveway, hoping to avoid Kyle seeing him.

Reaching into the pocket of his pants, he pulled out his Zippo and flicked it open, lighting it with one quick motion. It was something that he'd practiced for a long time until he'd gotten it right. Now, it seemed like such a trivial thing. He shrugged and lit the cigarette anyway, knowing how badly he needed it.

He walked further up toward Caleb's house, noticing there was a light on in the kitchen even though it was well past midnight. He knew his brother was probably not sleeping any more than he was.

He took one last drag of is cigarette and snuffed it out with the toe of his boot, and then walked up to the kitchen door. He knocked lightly, and while he waited for his brother to answer, he grabbed the slip of paper that was stuffed in the doorjamb.

Without waiting for Caleb to come to the door he tried the handle and it was unlocked. Caleb sat at the kitchen table, his head in his hands, and he appeared to be crying. Seth put a hand on his brother's shoulder to comfort him while trying not to get emotional himself. He sat down next to him and opened up the sheet of paper to show him.

"It looks like we got a ransom note after all," he said. "Someone put this in the doorjamb."

Caleb's head popped up, his eyes puffy and red, but he took the note and read it.

"She's put a message in it for me," he said, his eyes growing a little brighter.

He grabbed a notepad and a pen, and picked out the capitalized letters within her message, hoping to spell out her whereabouts. He scribbled the letters and showed it to Seth.

"Faith and Rachel."

"So she's with Faith?" Seth asked.

"There's more to it than that," Caleb said. "Felicia is the administrator of the orphanage. She isn't one of the nuns. The word, *sister*, stands out. What do you suppose she mean by that? Do you think she's figured out that Faith could be our sister?"

"It's sort of looks that way!" Seth said, feeling a bit of hope. "So now all we have to do is find Faith, and we'll probably find Amelia and the baby."

"The last line says more instructions will follow. That must mean she has more to tell us. But why would she be asking for half a million dollars? She probably couldn't put too much in one message, but that's probably a good thing. At least we know she's safe."

"She's safe as long as her kidnappers—whoever they are, don't catch on that we don't have that kind of money to give her."

"I don't think it's going to come to that," Caleb said. "If I know my wife, she's going to lead us right to her. In the meantime, let's call that detective and get him looking for her."

Chapter 12

"What time did the note get here?" The detective asked as he sipped the coffee Caleb got for him.

"I went out to smoke–uh, get some fresh air," Seth corrected himself. "It was around midnight. I saw the kitchen light on in the main house, so I came up to the door to see if Caleb was awake. That's when I noticed the note was stuffed in the doorjamb. We all parted ways around eight o'clock, so that's a four-hour window that he could've shown up."

The detective sighed as he took notes. "That doesn't give us much to go by. Your wife is smart for encrypting her message, but I hope it didn't put her at risk with her kidnappers. I know she wrote it by hand, and it's not as easily detected, but that doesn't mean she isn't risking her safety. Let's hope that finding this Faith woman is going to be the key, and we can put an end to all of this."

Seth could barely open his eyes when his cell phone started ringing beside him. The bright sun coming in through the window would have normally been enough to wake him, except that he and Kyle were up half the night plotting with Caleb to get his family back

"I'm going through the drive-thru to get a large coffee, can I come over and talk to you boys when I leave here?" the detective asked from the other end of the line.

"We'll be here," Seth said.

He pushed his feet to the floor and rubbed the sleep from his eyes, stretching his weary muscles.

He felt as if he'd run a marathon, the tension in his shoulders painful enough to make him reach for a bottle of ibuprofen at his bedside table. He popped a few in his mouth, and smoothed out the wrinkles in the shirt and pants he'd fallen asleep in, and shuffled his way toward the main house, where he hoped his brother would have a fresh pot of coffee ready.

No sooner had he sat down at the kitchen table with his brothers than the detective pulled up to the house.

Caleb greeted him at the door, and asked him to sit. He could tell by the look on his face that he didn't have good news for him.

"I wanted to talk to you boys together so there wouldn't be any misunderstanding," he said.

They all looked at each other, worry lining their faces.

"I'm afraid we haven't found Faith Miller," he began. "We checked her paperwork that she signed to identify her mother's body, and it gave an address for her and her husband, Zack Farmer.

The apartment looked like it was recently abandoned, and after talking to a few of their neighbors, it seems Zack lost his job recently, and they started hearing a lot of constant fighting. They also said Faith is pregnant, and that she'd be close to six months along by now."

"That's a lot of good information, but the only thing it helps is for us to understand that Mr. Farmer must have gone off the deep end when he lost his job, and thought kidnapping my sister-in-law and nephew and holding them for ransom was a good alternative for making money the honest way," Seth complained. "I know I have no room to talk because I used to have a gambling problem, but I didn't put a pregnant wife in the middle of a dangerous situation because of my selfishness."

"Where does our father, Zeb Yoder, fit into all of this?" Kyle asked.

"We haven't established a connection yet, since we've been unable to find him, so we don't know for sure if the two incidents are related."

He pulled out a couple of pictures from an envelope. "We were able to pull the video feed from the surveillance camera at the morgue when she went to submit to the DNA test to make an identification of the body that we excavated. We took a few stills from that video so at least we know what they look like."

Seth took the pictures of Faith. "She's Amish, and he's English!"

Kyle moved the picture up in front of Seth. "Do you see the resemblance?" he asked Caleb.

"The two of you could be twins!" he said.

He held the pictures out and studied them, realizing he couldn't deny the strong resemblance.

"Do you think she knows the old man is her father?" Kyle asked.

"You don't think they're working together, do you?" Caleb asked the detective.

"If I had to guess, I'd have to say her husband is the *brains and brawn* of this operation," he said. "According to the neighbors, she's always been very quiet and reserved, and he's become pretty aggressive with a temper. They suspected he started abusing her physically after he lost his job about three months ago. Faith doesn't fit the description of working with a seasoned criminal like your father."

"Sounds like he could be pretty dangerous if he decided to join forces with the old man!" Seth said. "And if she is our sister, he isn't going to get away with abusing her with us around!"

The detective put the pictures back into the manila envelope, and rose from his chair. "We put out an Amber alert with the description of his car and his license plate, so hopefully, he'll lead us to his new hideout. If you get a new ransom note, let us know, and we'll get right on it. In the meantime, I'm going to keep an officer out here on duty hoping we'll catch him when he tries to deliver the next note."

"That sounds like a good idea," Caleb said. "Thank you for all of your help."

He bid them a good morning, and was on his way. Caleb felt discouraged that they'd come up with nothing so far that would bring his beloved wife and son back home to him. He missed them dearly, and said a prayer that if Faith was his sister, and she was aware of it, that she would help Amelia escape unharmed.

Chapter 13

Zack looked at the final ransom note written by Amelia, pretending he could read it.

caleb,
On thursday, at 4pm,
Leave the money Down
inside the tunnel at the
new pavilion at Mans –
Field pARk on elM st.
~Amelia

"It looks good," he said. "I'm going into town to get a cheeseburger. I can't eat this *farm food* anymore. I can either take the two of you with me, or I can tie you to a chair. What'll it be?"

"I'd rather we went with you," Amelia offered.

Faith nodded, feeling a little uneasy about parading around in public with their *hostages*.

Once again, they piled into the dirty, rusted out Pontiac, and Amelia prayed it would backfire and draw attention from her own farm. Unfortunately, the strong breeze blowing in the afternoon storm would muffle the sound of the car from this distance with the rustling of the trees. If not for it being summer, she knew they would have been able to see the lights on last night from her kitchen window, but the thick cover of leaves on the trees camouflaged their presence from her family's view. The few acres between the two farms suddenly felt like a non-crossable border of a new country, making it seem further away than it really was.

When they pulled onto Main Street in town, Zack pulled up in front of the liquor store.

"Why are you stopping here, Zack?" Faith asked. "You promised you wouldn't drink anymore."

"Get off my back, Woman!" he said. "I'm not gonna drink. I'm looking for someone to deliver the ransom note."

It didn't take long for the owner of the store to kick out a few underage kids and yell at them for trying to buy beer.

"Bingo!" he said.

Zack opened the driver-side door, but turned to Faith before he exited the car. "Don't try anything funny. I'll be right there, and I'll be watching you!"

He pulled the keys from the ignition and walked toward the young boys, who were loitering near the entrance to the store.

"Hey boys," he said. "I just saw what happened. Why did he kick you out of the store? You're not causing trouble, are you?"

"No!" they all said together.

"He said my license was a fake, and refused to sell me some beer!" another one said.

"Let me see your license? He's got to be mistaken. Sounds to me like he's discriminating against you just for looking so young!"

The kid pulled out his wallet and handed Zack his license.

"That doesn't look like a fake, Mr. *Jones!*" he said. "But that doesn't help you since he isn't going to let you go back in there and get what you came here for. I'll tell you what. How about if I go in there and get you the beer?"

"Okay," they said together.

"I just need you to do me a favor first," Zack said, holding up the envelope containing the ransom note. "I need you to deliver this letter to a farm about ten miles down the road, and then I'll get you the beer."

"How do we know you'll still be here when we get back?" one of them asked.

"I'll give you twenty dollars, and then when you get back, I'll take my twenty dollars back, and you can give me the money to buy the beer. Then we can both be on our way!"

They took the money from him, and Zack waited until they were out of site to get back in his car.

"Did I hear you tell those boys you'd buy them beer for delivering that note?" Amelia asked.

"Yeah, so what?" he said casually, as he started his car and revved the engine to keep it from stalling.

"Those boys aren't old enough to drink!" she said angrily. "Why would you promise them you'd get them beer?"

Zack turned around in the seat and leered at her.

"Get off my back! I'm not going to justify myself to you!" he said, gritting his teeth at her. "I don't have any intention of getting those kids any beer. They ain't old enough to drink, and they're trying to use a fake license to buy beer."

"Then why did you promise them you would?"

"So they would deliver the note!" he said, putting the car in reverse and backing out of the parking spot. "I have a feeling they're gonna get caught delivering that note, and they might get arrested, and hopefully that'll scare 'em straight! I wished I'd had a chance to learn that lesson when I was their age, b'cause then maybe I wouldn't have turned out the way I did."

"So you're sending them into the lion's den?" Amelia asked.

"If you mean, I'm letting them take the fall for this, then yes!" he answered. "By the time the cops catch up to those kids, we'll be long gone from here," he said, as he squealed his tires and sped toward the old man's farm, forgetting all about the cheeseburger he'd claimed he couldn't live without, but Amelia had a hunch he'd just given those boys his last dollar, and he was in for a rude awakening when he discovered there wouldn't be any ransom money.

Chapter 14

Zeb cringed at the mess that someone—squatters perhaps, had left in his house since he'd been gone.

Was it too much to expect that his son would take care of the place in his absence and run off any low-life moochers trying to take his land from him?

He moved about slowly, still weak from being in a coma for so many months. His muscles had all but completely atrophied, and he wasn't certain how much further he would have made it if not for the kindness of the young boys who'd offered him a ride.

Within minutes, he could hear sirens, and for some reason, he just wasn't afraid this time. He'd had enough of running; his only goal was to see the Bishop for his confession—his last confession.

Uncertain if he'd even make it much longer in this life, he needed redemption more than ever.

But now, with the police closing in on him, he didn't hold out much hope of getting to see the Bishop before he was caught.

"I suppose it's your will, Lord," he mumbled. "But you know I need forgiveness in this life if I want to go on to the next life, and you know my days here are few. I can feel the end is near for me. Please give me a sign that I can receive the redemption I desperately need."

It had been so long since he'd breathed such a sincere prayer; he'd forgotten how liberating it could be.

He peered out the side window, noting that the young boys who'd given him a ride had been stopped by the police, and he knew it would only be a matter of time before they would be at his home to arrest him and take him back to jail.

He didn't think he'd make it even one day in jail. His energy was spent and he'd become so frail while he'd been sick, he was surprised he'd even survived the fall into his cellar, let alone the drowning.

He'd never forget the deep sadness he'd experienced when he'd felt his life slipping away. It had filled him with a lot of regrets—mostly over not raising his children right. He'd finally realized what a gift they were, and now they would never know how much he regretted not bringing them up with a good example. He'd spent his entire life only thinking of himself, and mourning the loss of the community and his standing in the eyes of the Bishop—a mere man, that he'd missed out on the most important thing in this life—to know his Savior.

When he'd been in a coma, someone—a minister, perhaps, had visited his bedside regularly and had read to him from the Bible, and he'd heard the word of God, and understood what it meant for the first time in his life. He knew then that he had to get well and make amends to everyone he'd wronged—somehow he had to.

Chapter 15

"I already told you, officer," the boy said. "This guy gave us twenty dollars to drop off a note for him. He told us to put it in the mailbox. That's all, I swear!"

"What did he look like?" the officer demanded.

"He was kind of tall and had dark hair," the boy said. "I saw him get into a gold colored car with two other girls—oh, and there was a baby crying!"

The officer held up the pictures of Faith and asked if that was one of the women.

"I think so," the boy said. "I can't be sure."

When he showed him the surveillance pictures of Zack, he was able to make a positive identification.

"I'm going to need you to go down to the station and give a full statement.

"I'm not going to the juvey, am I?"

"At seventeen, you won't go to the juvenile center; you'll go to jail if you're involved. That man kidnapped a woman and her child!"

All the boys in the car began to fight with the driver, blaming him for agreeing to take the note.

"We didn't help anyone kidnap anyone," one of them said. "We just wanted some beer, and he was going to buy it for us. He just wanted us to deliver the note first. Honest."

"Beer?" the officer said. "Now you're all under arrest for attempting to buy alcoholic beverages, and for being an accessory to kidnapping!"

The officers made all four boys get out of the car, and then they read them their rights and handcuffed them, putting them in the back of two patrol cars.

Zeb watched the boys being taken away, feeling relief that it wasn't him, and that whatever they had done wrong, that they had spared his life.

"I promise you, Lord," he declared. "Since you've given me this second chance, I'll do whatever it is that you need me to. I want forgiveness that much!"

Chapter 16

Zeb peered out the window of the living room when he heard a car coming up the long gravel drive that led to his house. It was an older, gold car—not one he recognized.

Instinctively, he went to the closet in the hallway and stomped on the floorboard in the corner with his heel. The plank flipped up, and he reached in to retrieve his shotgun and a box of shells. He quickly loaded the gun and stuffed a few extra shells in the pocket of his trousers, and then closed himself inside the closet.

He found himself praying again that God would guard him from further sin, and that he would not have to use the gun to defend himself. In his weakened state, it was his only defense against intruders, but for the first time in too many years, he felt God had heard his prayer.

A loud, male voice caused his heart to jump.

"It won't be long now, Amish girl," Zack said. "And I'll have the money, and as long as you cooperate, I'll set you free."

"What is that supposed to mean?" Faith cried. "You promised you wouldn't hurt Amelia and her baby!"

Zeb sucked in his breath. Were they talking about Caleb's Amelia? The mention of a baby was a surprise to him. He'd never thought of the possibility of being a grandfather. From the sound of things, they were in danger, but he decided to listen a little more to see if he could figure out what their plan was, and how many he was up against.

"Shut up, Faith!" Zack said.

Faith?

"I told you not to get emotional over this. The old man wasn't emotional when he poisoned your mother with that tea. Now his son's wife and kid are gonna have to pay if we don't get the money from that robbery he committed!"

Zeb had no idea who that man was that he heard, but he now knew it was his own daughter that was in danger, as well as his son's wife, and his own grandchild.

He had to save his family!

He breathed a prayer for courage as he burst out of the closet, shotgun ready for whatever he needed to do.

Both women screamed, and Zack held up his arms in defense.

"Zeb," Amelia said. "What are you doing here?"

He aimed the gun at Zack and raised it as if to threaten him. "I could ask this one the same thing! From the sound of things, you're up to no good, and you seem to have yourself a hostage situation here. I can't let you do that, Son. I'm not going to let you hurt my girls, or my grandchild."

Amelia's breath hitched. "Girls?" she asked.

"Faith is my daughter!"

Zack took a step forward. "She's not your daughter! She wouldn't be kin to no murderer!"

Zeb looked at Faith's swelling belly and then back at Zack. "Well, from what I can see, she's going to be *married* to a murderer if you aim to do any of them harm. I'm afraid I just can't allow that!"

"What are you going to do, old man? Shoot me?"

"If you force me to, yes!" he said. "Girls, I have some good strong rope in the kitchen on a hook by the door. Tie him up!"

Faith wiped the tears from her eyes, wondering why she was getting so emotional. Was it that she finally knew who her real father was? Perhaps disappointment at what kind of a man he was? Or maybe, just maybe, it was relief that he was sparing her and her unborn child from going to jail for her husband's foolishness.

Her emotions were overwhelming, but she did as she was told. He was, after all, her father.

Chapter 17

Caleb read the note one more time and confirmed to the officers that Amelia was being held at his father's home. Though the old man had not been mentioned, he still worried he was involved somehow.

"You stay put," the detective warned Caleb and his brothers. "You'll only be in the way, and as tough as this is to trust us, this is what we do. Be patient, and say a few prayers that we'll be back here in no time with your son and your wife."

"We will," he answered, looking at his brothers in a challenging way.

He watched the officers leave, and then stepped over to the kitchen window straining to see through the thick of the trees. The officers snaked their way over to the house, and Caleb prayed their presence wouldn't spook the kidnappers.

His brothers stood next to him and prayed quietly, but all he could concentrate on was the scene unfolding in his backyard.

Resisting the urge to run over there when he saw that the officers were encroaching on his father's property, Caleb felt his throat constricting, his face covered in perspiration as if he'd plowed his entire cornfield in one afternoon.

"Go on now," Zeb told the girls. "Go get help and I'll hold him here until you get back here with Caleb and his brothers."

"I don't want to leave my husband here with you," Faith said. "I don't want you to hurt him!"

"I won't hurt him," he promised. "I give you my word. But before you go, I want you both to know how sorry I am for everything I've done to hurt you, and my sons—and your mothers."

Amelia looked at him, tears welling up in her eyes. "I believe you," she said softly. "I forgive you, and I know Caleb does too."

Faith began to cry. "If she can forgive you, then so can I. What about you, Zack?"

"I don't know if I'm ready to forgive," he said. "But I'm ready to surrender. No amount of money is worth dying for, and I don't trust this old man! Get me out of here!"

Faith went to him, sobbing and giggling slightly. She looked up at Zeb with a pleading gleam in her eyes.

"Is it okay to untie him?"

He nodded. "On one condition."

"You name it," Zack said.

"I may not be around much longer, and I want you to take good care of my daughter, and my grandchild she's carrying."

Zack hung his head. "But I lost my job! I can't even pay for our rent, let alone for the birth!"

"I'm willing to take the blame for this kidnapping because I'm going to spend the rest of my life in jail for other crimes I'm not proud of, which means my house will just sit here."

He turned to Faith. "With Amelia as a witness, I'm willing to give you my house, but only if your husband promises to work hard and take care of you and the baby. There isn't any money for you to gain from this, only *familye,* and that can be worth far more than money. I regret that I didn't learn that until now!"

Zack's eyes lit up. "I'd appreciate that, Sir," he said. "But I gave the ransom note to those boys to deliver. They can identify me!"

"What did the notes say?" Zeb asked.

Amelia told him, and he chuckled.

"Were they full of code messages, the way you and Caleb used to write when you were children? The messages you sent with the pigeons?"

She smiled. "How did you know?"

"I found them on the floor of his room. He never picked it up when he was young. And I soon learned to break your code!"

"So then you know that, by now, Caleb knows where we are, and the police are probably on their way here," she said.

Zeb nodded. "That means we don't have much time. I'll tell the police I was holding you against your will and that I made you write the notes. I'm willing to take all the blame, if you agree to start fresh and be a good husband and father—not like me!"

Zack nodded. "I give you my word. Thank you for taking the blame for my mistake. I don't know what I was thinking. I lost my head because of the stress I was under when I lost my job and our apartment. We've been living in the car for two weeks."

"You have a house now. Don't mess this up!" Zeb warned. "I can see in my daughter's eyes that she believes in you. I don't think you're a bad man like me; I just think that you're a mixed up young man who's lost his way, and I pray that giving you a way out of the mess you created will set you on the right path again."

Still tied up, Zack turned his attention to Amelia. "I'm truly sorry for what I did. I'll do my best to do right by you and your family."

"We're *your* family now. I'm sure my husband and his brothers will want you to work with them now that they have a sister to look after."

The two women hugged. "I've always wanted a sister," Amelia said.

"Me too!" Faith agreed.

Faith untied her husband, and he kissed her and apologized for letting stress turn him abusive against her, promising not to let it happen again.

The three of them walked out of the house, Amelia holding Gabriel close to her heart.

No sooner did they get out the door, than the police closed in on them.

"Stop where you are!" one of them said.

Zack threw his hands up and dropped to his knees. "Don't shoot!"

Chapter 18

Caleb ran from the house when he saw Amelia exiting his father's home. He'd been so afraid and so overwhelmed, that tears now streamed down his face as he ran the length of the field. In the time that his father had been in a coma, Caleb and his brothers had torn down all the barbed wire and electric fence that had separated the two farms.

Now, he ran freely through the corn field full of thick, healthy stalks he'd planted with his brothers.

Amelia heard Caleb calling for her from the cornfield, and for the first time, she did not fear the maze of rows she could not see through. She trusted, as she followed the calls of her future that echoed over the silk tassels swaying in the warm summer breeze that felt refreshing against her cheeks.

The barriers were down, and perhaps now they would truly be free to live their lives without the fear of the past. There were no more ghosts that called to her from within the rows that confined her; she heard only the sweet sound of her husband's voice calling her.

When she reached his waiting arms, a shield of safety surrounded her in the warmth of his embrace.

"I was so frightened," he said, as his lips ran across the top of his wife's head until they found her lips.

"We're fine," she reassured him. "Our troubles are over—finally!"

"How can you be sure?" he asked, pulling his son into his arms and searching his wife's eyes.

"Your *daed* has asked for forgiveness, and he's willing to change his life around. He's found *Gott* again!"

Caleb's eyes teared up all over again, and his lower lip quivered, slowly turning into a smile.

"That's wonderful news," he said, realizing his father had been behind the abduction.

It no longer mattered. If his father was looking for forgiveness, Caleb would give it to him freely.

Chapter 19

Amelia found Caleb's hand and pulled him back through the cornfield toward the other side.

"Come with me," she said. "There's someone I want you to meet!"

They walked hand-in-hand through the length of the field toward his father's home.

When they reached the perimeter, Caleb stopped to watch police officers putting his father into the back of a patrol car. It was a scene he wasn't sure he would ever get used to, but it was a reality he'd have to learn to accept.

He dropped his hand from Amelia's and went to the car, still holding his son in his arms.

"May I talk to my father before you go?"

The officer nodded and opened the back door to his patrol car.

Caleb peered in at his father, who was pale and thin. It saddened him to see the man in such a state, but he'd brought it all on himself.

"I'd like you to meet my son, Gabriel," Caleb said to his father.

"I saw him, Son," he said, with a shaky voice. "I want you to know how proud I am of the man you've turned out to be, and I thank *Gott* that you did not follow in my footsteps. You're a *gut mann,* Caleb, and so are your brothers. I'm sorry for everything I've done to you and everyone else. I know it doesn't change what happened, or take back any of the consequences of my selfish behavior, but I pray that you learn from it, and promise to always listen to *Gott. "*

"I will," Caleb said, swallowing back tears. "I want you to know, *daed,* that I love you, no matter what. And I forgive you."

"That means a lot to me, Caleb—probably more than you could ever know."

By this time, Seth and Kyle had reached the farm, and each wanted to talk to their father.

Each of them accepted his apology, and blessed him with the gift of the forgiveness he so desperately needed. He'd confessed to the police officers before they'd taken him from his house, and the truth had finally set him free. There were no more shackles of guilt that weighed on his heart. No more ghosts of the past taunting him back to his sinful ways.

His sins had been confessed and forgiven.

It was all he needed, before taking his last breath.

Chapter 20

Zack took a deep breath in and blew it out slowly. It was good to get all that off his chest. He knew that by the old man's example, he had to accept responsibility for his actions, and to be willing to accept the consequences, whatever that may be.

Caleb lifted his head from the deep prayer he'd been engrossed in while he'd listened to Zack's confession.

"I think I can speak for each of my brothers, that we will leave this alone. Our father has accepted the blame for all of this, and he blessed you with a gift; the gift of a clean slate. He'd accepted the responsibility and took your mistake on himself in order that his daughter, our sister, would have a better life, and you both could have a fresh start. We, as a family, will take care of you, and help you in any way. You're more than welcome to work with my brothers and me, and you're free to live on the old man's farm the way he gifted it to you. There's been enough death and destruction in this family, and it's up to us—the blessed ones, to make a new path for our children, and to leave them with a better heritage than was left to us."

"I couldn't agree more," Kyle said.

Zack teared up, and thanked each of them, realizing how truly blessed he was.

They were all blessed to be the children of a repentant and forgiven man.

Seth leaned in close to Zack. "There's one last thing I want to make clear. If we ever see another mark on our sister, or even so much as a look in her eyes that makes us *think* you're not treating her right, my brothers and I will take you out to the woodshed and have a nice long *talk* with you," he whispered. "Do we understand each other?"

Zack nodded his head, and Seth slapped him on the back and pulled him into a man-hug.

"Well, then welcome to the family!"

THE END

Thank you for reading this suspense series. Please leave a review on Amazon and let me know how much you enjoyed it. I always love hearing from my readers.

God Bless!

Please enjoy a sneak preview of The Anniversary:

CHAPTER 1

"Sadie, girl," a familiar voice called out.

Fear rippled through Sadie like ice water slowing the blood flow in her veins.

Her mother had been the only one to ever call her that, and she'd been dead for seven years.

In the dark, she could hear people shuffling around while teenage girls screamed. Sadie hadn't remembered seeing any young girls at the party when she and Sam walked into the country club.

"Sadie, girl. Where are you?"

Sadie's pulse raced. That was indeed her mother's voice, but how could that be? Her heart beat fast at the thought of it.

She struggled to see as lightning flashed, illuminating the room for a few seconds. Thunder rumbled, and more screams interrupted the silent, slow-motion of her thoughts.

Just minutes ago, she'd been on the dance floor arguing with her husband, Sam, about whose fault it was that their marriage had fallen apart. She'd told him she wished they could go back fifty years ago to the night they met to prove which of them had asked the other to dance in the first place. And then lightning flashed brighter than she'd even seen; thunder rattled the building like an earthquake. The power had gone out, and she couldn't see anything in the country club.

What was happening?

"Sadie, girl. Where are you?" her mother's voice called out to her again.

Sadie's heart beat so loudly, she could hear it beating among the chaos, but her feet wouldn't move.

Someone bumped into her and grasped her arm.

"Sadie Marie, your momma's calling you. You better answer her before she grounds you."

"Who's there?" Sadie's weak voice trembled as she spoke.

"It's me, Eleanor, your best friend, silly."

Eleanor had passed away almost a year ago from complications after she broke her hip. What was going on? Was this some sort of cruel anniversary joke Sam was playing on her? And where *was* Sam? Why wasn't he beside her? Hadn't they just been dancing before the lightning knocked the power out?

Maybe I was struck by the lightning and I'm passed out dead on the floor, or this is one very realistic dream. God, please be with me. I'm scared.

"Sadie Marie Hall, answer me this minute."

Eleanor nudged her arm. "Sadie, you better answer your momma. She used your full name."

"But my mother couldn't possibly be calling me because she's dead. And my last name isn't Hall anymore. It's Livingston." The words came out slowly, as Sadie struggled to make some sense of what was happening.

Lightning flashed again, and Sadie nearly passed out when she saw young Eleanor standing next to her.

Eleanor steadied her friend. "That's not funny to say your mother's dead. And your name is Sadie Marie Hall. Has been your entire life. You're not supposed to change your name until you get married, silly."

"But I *am* married. I've been married to Sam for fifty years. We have two children."

"That's impossible. You're only going to be eighteen next week. You're too young to be married, and most certainly too young to be a momma."

Sadie was growing impatient with this practical joke. "I'm going to be *sixty-eight* next week *not* eighteen!"

"Very funny, Sadie. My grandmother is that old, and she tells me all the time how much she hates it, so why would you want to be so quick to go from being a teenager to being over the hill?"

Sadie put her hand to her stomach thinking she was going to be sick. "I'm so thin! What happened to me? And why is my skirt so short?"

Before they'd left the house for their anniversary party, Sadie and Sam had each surprised each other by wearing a remake of the outfits they'd worn on their first date, hoping it would rekindle a spark in their otherwise estranged relationship. They'd even had the idea to recreate the scene at the country club for their fiftieth wedding anniversary party. She'd felt old and frumpy as she'd stared at her reflection in the vintage clothes, but now that image seemed to have changed.

Eleanor pulled on Sadie's arm. "I think you need to sit down for a minute. You must have bumped your head when the lights went out."

In the background, she could still hear her mother somewhere in the dark room, asking repeatedly if anyone had seen her. No one seemed to be answering her.

Sadie plopped down hard in a wooden folding chair. She placed a hand on the chair, realizing she was no longer in the country club. They didn't have wooden folding chairs in the ballroom; they had red, velvet cushioned chairs, and the round tables had table cloths. The table she leaned her arm on now was wooden.

"Am I dead? Is that why I'm able to see you, and hear my mother? Where are we?"

She felt the goose bumps on her arms, noticing how thin her arms felt.

"We're at the Fruitport Pavilion. We came straight over from graduation. Don't you remember?"

That was where she'd met Sam—the night she'd graduated from Marywood Academy. She had planned to go to college at the end of the summer, but she'd met Sam and married him instead.

"That was fifty years ago. The Fruitport Pavilion burned down Christmas Eve of '62."

"That's a year and a half from now, Sadie. You aren't making any sense. You must have bumped your head harder than I thought. I'll get your dad. He'll know what to do."

Sadie grabbed Eleanor's arm. "My father shouldn't be here—wherever *here* is. He's still alive?"

Eleanor sat down beside her. "Do you think I'm dead, too?"

"I sat by your hospital bed after your surgery and…"

As the lightning flashed, she could see the panic in her young friend's eyes, and she just couldn't bring herself to say another word.

"Maybe we should just sit here quietly until the lights come back on. Are you dizzy or anything?"

Sadie put a hand to her head to feel if there were any bumps. "I think I'm fine. But maybe you're right and we should just sit here for a minute and think."

Off in the distance, a siren could be heard—but it sounded funny. Almost the same as it would have when she was a young girl. It wasn't a modern sounding siren; it was way too old-fashioned. Through the windows, she could see flashes of the white, station wagon ambulance pull up to the building while the lightning flickered in the dark. The large, round light on the roof hypnotized Sadie as it flashed its red light through the windows.

Eleanor gave her arm a squeeze. "Are you sure you're fine, because you're being too quiet."

I'm probably dead, but other than that I'm fine.

Sadie turned to her friend. "What year is it?"

Eleanor nudged her. "It's 1961. The same as it was when you woke up this morning, silly."

Sadie could feel the blood draining from her face. "Eleanor, I know you're not going to believe me, but when I woke up this morning, it was the year 2011!"

Eleanor laughed. "That's impossible. We will be living on the moon by then. The astronauts are planning a trip to the moon, and LIFE Magazine says we could be living on the moon in the future."

Sadie had to interrupt her. "Trust me when I tell you that we will *not* be living on the moon in the future, but I can't talk about this now; I have to find Sam."

"Oh yeah; your *husband.*" Eleanor rolled her eyes.

Sadie couldn't worry about the disbelief in Eleanor's tone. She had to find Sam quickly so she could put an end to this nightmare.

Eleanor followed closely on her heels as she waded carefully through the crowd calling out for Sam.

"Sadie, girl, is that you?" her mother was calling her each time she called out for Sam, her voice growing near.

"Not now, Mother," Sadie surprised herself by spouting off in such a tone. "I have to find Sam, and I will deal with you later since I'm only imagining you."

"Sadie Marie Hall, you come here this minute or…"

Sadie continued to push through the crowd, her mother on her heels. "Or what, Mother? You'll ground me until I'm eighteen? Well you're too late for that!"

She is not real. Do not turn around. Just keep walking so you can find Sam and get out of this nightmare.

Sadie moved further into the crowd, continuing to call out to Sam.

"He's over here," a young boy's voice rang out from the crowd.

Sadie moved quickly toward the sound of the voice, until the lights suddenly came on. Sadie froze when she saw young Sam being lifted onto the stretcher, blood staining the side of his face. In the background, she could hear muffled sounds of the crowd around her cheering as they patted a maintenance man on the shoulder for restoring the lights. She scanned the room, realizing she was in the Fruitport Pavilion instead of the country club. Nearly losing her footing, she stumbled backward into a chair.

One of the paramedics looked up at her. "Are you hurt, Miss?"

Miss? I'm old enough to be your mother.

She pointed to Sam, who was lying lifelessly on the stretcher, his thick hair devoid of any gray. Short sideburns graced the side of his youthful face, his chin resting on the narrow lapel of his suit. His thin, black tie lay crumpled on the floor, and Sadie bent down to pick it up.

"Is Sam dead?"

"No, Miss. He's unconscious, so we need to get him to the hospital. He probably has a concussion. You say his name is Sam? Do you know his last name and birth date?"

Sadie lifted herself from the chair; her legs still feeling wobbly. "His last name is Livingston and he'd be eighteen now. His birthday was March fifteen. I have to go with him."

One of the paramedics held a hand up to stop her.

"I'm sorry Miss, but only family can go with him."

"I'm his wife!"

Both paramedics looked her over and snickered.

"You two aren't old enough to be married. Move aside so we can get this boy to the hospital."

Tears filled Sadie's eyes as she watched the paramedics cart Sam away, leaving her there like she was unimportant.

Eleanor grabbed her arm. "How do you know so much about that boy? He doesn't go to our school, so how do you know him when I know nothing about it?"

Sadie felt numb. She couldn't answer her friend any more than she could run after the paramedics and insist she go to the hospital with Sam. She could sense her mother was right behind her.

"Sadie girl, there you are. Why didn't you stop when I was calling you?" Her mother's voice was so close she could feel her breath on the back of neck.

Sadie hesitated before turning to face her mother. Feeling truly afraid she might faint at the sight of her dead mother, she took a deep breath, and then another before facing her.

Panic rose up in Sadie's throat as she looked at her mother's feet; they were so dainty in her pointed-toe stilettos. Her thin legs were wrapped in thick stockings—not sheer like modern pantyhose. The conservative, brown-tweed dress rested just below her knees; the buttoned front adorned with a cream-colored collar. Her deep auburn hair touched her shoulders, flipping upward at the ends, and her roots had been teased to give it height. Slight creases framed her smile, and her youthful face showed a hint of freckles most likely the result of time spent in her flower garden.

Sadie's eyes filled with tears at the sight of her mother. She looked so young, it nearly took her breath away.

"Sadie girl, are you okay?"

Sadie allowed tears to fall from her eyes, not daring to blink, for fear her mother would disappear. Her mother pulled her toward her, and she threw herself into her mother's arms, crying uncontrollably.

"It's so good to see you again, mom."

Memories of her mother in her younger years flooded Sadie's mind as she breathed in the gentle scent of Jean Nate on her mother's collar. It was a comforting smell that had always stayed with her.

"I've been here the whole night," her mother said as she smoothed back Sadie's hair. "This was obviously not the kind of celebration we had in mind for your graduation, so let's get you home and into bed."

Graduation? I'm just happy to see you again—even if you're not real. But home sounds really good right now because I'm not ready to let you go just yet.

CHAPTER 2

Sadie stirred just a little, trying to hold onto the vivid memory of her mother before she woke fully. Her head ached at the thought of the nightmare she'd had, even though some parts of her dream were very pleasant. She could still smell the faint aroma of her mother's perfume as she rolled over in her bed. She kept her eyes closed, allowing the scent to linger in her memory for as long as she could keep it there. The sting of reality was more than she could handle. She wasn't ready to lose her mother all over again, and she knew it was eminent the moment she opened her eyes to the present.

The scent of fresh coffee drifted through her nostrils, and she could almost hear the faint sound of her mother's percolator brewing. She pushed her head under the pillow, trying to drown out the sound she knew was only in her head. She was fully awake, and still hadn't opened her eyes for fear that her reality was not what she wanted it to be at the moment. In her head she knew Sam was brewing the coffee, but her heart wanted so much for it to be her mother.

Oh mom, I didn't realize I was still missing you so much. God, please don't take her away from me a second time.

Taking a chance, she opened her eyes slowly, filtering the sunlight through her long eyelashes. As her childhood room came into focus, her heart slammed against her chest wall. Sadie tried to blink away the realization of where she was, but she couldn't make it go away. Her heartbeat pounded so loudly, she could hear nothing else. She closed her eyes again and took a deep breath.

Just breathe. Let me think about this for a minute. I must still be dreaming. Or I could be dead. Of course I could be having a bad reaction to medication. Or I could be dead. There has to be a logical explanation for why I'm in my room at my parent's house. I must be dead.

Sadie sat up in the bed and opened her eyes again, willing herself to accept whatever the situation was. Her hand fell to the chenille bedspread as she looked at her collection of records next to her record player on the metal cart beside her vanity dressing table. She craned her neck to get a glimpse of herself in the mirror above the dressing table, and nearly fell off the bed. She sprang from the bed, her focus on her face. She moved in closer to the image staring back at her in the mirror, her reflection startling. Instinctively, her hand went to her face as she surveyed her smooth skin. Not one wrinkle invaded her face, and her hair, though messy, did not contain even one gray strand.

She giggled madly, wondering if she blinked would her reflection turn old again. Testing her theory, she closed her eyes, the memory of her younger self taunting her. Sadie took a deep breath and counted to three, hoping that would be enough. When she opened her eyes, she was delighted to see the eighteen-year-old version of herself staring back at her.

Less than thirty-six hours ago she'd stared at her older self in the mirror wearing a tailor-made replica of this same outfit. Remembering how foolish she'd felt wearing the pencil skirt that clung to her ample figure, she could only admire how much thinner she looked in it now. Sure the linen skirt was badly wrinkled from sleeping in it, but she'd been too tired to worry past collapsing on the bed when her parents had brought her home last night.

Her mind drifted to events that led up to the point when she'd changed and become young again. While waiting for Sam to come home on the night of their fiftieth wedding anniversary, she'd looked at her watch seven times in the span of five minutes, wondering why he couldn't manage to make it home early just one night. It had angered her that he disregarded her the way he had in recent years, always putting her needs last. She'd made a mental list of things she would do over again if given the chance. She'd actually wished—prayed for a *do-over*.

When they'd arrived at the country club, she was delighted to see that he'd taken the time to have the ballroom decorated to match the Fruitport Pavilion on the pier at Spring Lake. The place where they'd first met, and shared their first dance. But it wasn't enough to make up for her feelings of estrangement toward him for so many years. They'd argued over which one of them had asked the other to dance. And just before the lights went out, they'd both said that they wished they could go back to that night and undo their first meeting.

If this was God's way of teaching them both a lesson for wishing such a thing, she wondered why she hadn't wished for it before now. For whatever reason; she young again, and she intended to discover why.

She continued to revel in her youthful reflection until a knock sounded at the door. Her eyes grew wide, and her heart beat faster when her mother called her from the other side of the door. Her response caught in her throat, choking her with the lump that quickly formed from the hope that rose up in her. She plunked herself down on her bed, fearing she would faint.

If I answer her will I sound young or old? If I'm hallucinating, will she go away if I don't answer?

"Sadie girl, are you awake?" Her mother's voice carried a little impatience in her tone.

"Yes, ma'am," she mumbled.

The crystal doorknob twisted, squeaking the way Sadie remembered. Her mother entered the room, and she couldn't help but stare into her chocolate-brown eyes. As she had aged, they'd become dull and dark, but looking into them now reminded her of a chocolate river, sparkling in the sunlight. Her presence gave Sadie a sense of order and comfort that only a mother could give.

She sat up straight as her mother picked up the dress Sadie had left on the floor. "Are you feeling better this morning?"

Well that's a loaded question, mom. I'm feeling young, and afraid; excited and confused all at once.

Sadie nodded, unable to push any words from her throat. She smiled as she watched her mother fuss with laundry in her room.

I'm old enough to take care of my laundry myself. You don't have to pick up after me anymore.

She felt sorry for her mother, remembering how much she took her for granted when she was young. Hopping off her bed, she took the things from her mother and set them in the hamper inside the closet.

Her mother looked at her funny. "Are you sure you didn't bump your head last night? Your father can take a look if you need him to."

Maybe I will talk to Daddy. He's probably still a doctor. That much probably hasn't changed. He should know what happened and how to fix this. I hope."

Sadie shrugged, feeling suddenly unsure.

Her mother sat on the edge of the bed. "Well now you're making me worry."

Sadie kissed her mother on the top of her head. "Don't worry, Mom. I do feel a little funny after last night. Something isn't right and I don't know what it is, but I'm sure Daddy will know what to do."

Annie Hall tugged on her daughter's arm. "I'm sure you're right. Change your clothes and come down to breakfast. I'm sure your father will keep his nose out of the morning paper long enough to talk to you about whatever is bothering you."

Her ten-year-old brother, Max came whirling into her room just then. She stared at him, remembering they were so many years apart they'd never had a close relationship.

"I hear your brain got fried in last night's lightning storm," Max teased her.

Her mother shooed him with her hand. "Leave your sister alone, Max, and go eat your breakfast."

Max stuck his tongue out at Sadie before leaving the room. She could hear him thump down every step before jumping down to the landing. Her mother exited the room then, leaving her alone to get dressed for Sunday breakfast with her family—something she missed more than she realized until now.

Sadie pulled a pink dress and a cashmere sweater from the closet, and then pulled her hair back into a high ponytail. She found a matching ribbon on her dressing table and tied it in her hair. She felt funny as she pulled on a pair of bobby socks and tied her saddle shoes. She did, however, admire how thin she was again. That was the one thing she'd regretted over the years—letting herself put on thirty-something pounds from emotional eating. Comfort food that had kept her company while Sam worked their lives away.

I forgot about Sam. I have to find him and try to make sense of what's happening to me. To us.

At the dining room table, Sadie sat in her usual spot next to Max. He was emptying several spoons-full of Tang into his glass of water. The table was filled with plates of homemade pecan waffles, scrambled eggs, bacon, and blueberry muffins. She'd forgotten how much she loved her mother's pecan waffles and homemade syrup that was always thick and warm. Her mother filled her plate as she sat there, stunned.

Sadie put up a hand, hoping to reduce the amount of food being piled on her plate. "I haven't eaten bacon in years. Not since my cholesterol is too high."

Her father shook his head at her. "What are you talking about, Sadie Marie? We had bacon for breakfast yesterday,"

Sadie cleared her throat. "Nothing, Daddy. I'm just being silly."

Her mother poured her a glass of water from the pitcher that sat on the table.

"Is that filtered water, Mom?"

She regretted the words as soon as they left her mouth.

Her mother smiled oddly. "What do you mean, *filtered water,* Sadie girl?"

Sadie paused for a minute, trying to find the right words to say. "It's nothing, Mom. Don't pay any attention to anything I'm saying. I'm confused or I'm having a bad case of PMS."

Her mother sat across from her, confusion distorting her face. "Sadie girl, what are you talking about? What's PMS?"

Sadie shoved a piece of bacon in her mouth to avoid answering her mother.

I need to just stop talking because everything that comes out of my mouth is wrong. She's going to have me committed to the asylum if I'm not careful.

Her mother pushed at her husband's newspaper. "Stewart, do you know what Sadie Marie is talking about? I think she must have hit her head last night because she isn't making any sense, and I'm worried about her. Will you please have a look at her?"

Sadie wiped her mouth with her napkin and started to push herself away from the table. "May I be excused? I'm fine—really. I just need to talk to Eleanor, and I have to go see Sam at the hospital. Can I borrow the car, Daddy?"

Her mother wagged her finger at her. "Sadie girl, you don't know how to drive, and you don't have an operator's license. Your father and I are willing to overlook your behavior last night because of all the excitement, but asking to borrow the car is a bit over the top. Don't you think so, Stewart? "

Sadie turned to her father, who seemed amused by the banter between her and her mother. "Daddy, please let me borrow the car. Mine isn't here—I'm not really sure where it is, but I *do* know how to drive, and I *do* have a license. None of this matters anyway because none of this is real. So if I wreck the car it won't really be wrecked. All I want to do right now is see Sam so I can get out of this wacky nightmare. I love you guys, but you're just not real."

Her father reached into his pocket and handed her the keys, a smirk showing on his face.

"Stewart, you can't be serious? It's too dangerous for her to drive when you haven't taught her yet. Didn't you hear how strange she's sounding? She thinks she has her own car."

She snatched the keys from her father's hands before her mother could get her hands on them. Then she placed a kiss on each of her parents' cheeks and told them she loved them. As she ran out the door, her mother called after her.

"Be careful, Sadie girl. And who is Sam?"

Sadie waved goodbye to her mother and hopped into the car without answering her. She didn't dare look back, but she knew the woman would stand in the driveway until she was out of sight, and her expression would continue to wear a deep fluster.

This is the end of the preview for The Anniversary. If you would like to continue to read it, you may purchase it on Kindle or paperback on Amazon.

Thank you, and Happy Reading!